A Paw-some Mystery

Adapted by Mary Man-Kong
Based on the screenplay by Amy Wolfram
Illustrated by Lora Lee

Special thanks to Venetia Davie, Ryan Ferguson, Charnita Belcher, Tanya Mann, Julia Phelps, Sharon Woloszyk, Nicole Corse, Darren Sander, Rita Lichtwardt, Carla Alford, Julia Pistor, Renata Marchand, Michelle Cogan, ARC Productions and Michael Goguen

A Random House PICTUREBACK® Book

Random House 🏠 New York

Published in the United States by Random House Children's Books, a division of Penguin Random House LLC, 1745 Broadway, New York, NY 10019, and in Canada by Random House of Canada, a division of Penguin Random House Ltd., Toronto. No part of this book may be reproduced or copied in any form without permission from the copyright owner. Pictureback, Random House, and the Random House colophon are registered trademarks of Penguin Random House LLC.
ISBN 978-0-553-52448-2 (pbk) — ISBN 978-0-553-52449-9 (ebook)
randomhousekids.com
Printed in the United States of America
10 9 8 7 6 5 4 3 2 1

Barbie, Skipper, Stacie, and Chelsea couldn't wait!
The sisters were going to visit Grandma Roberts for
two weeks in their hometown of Willows, Wisconsin.

When they arrived, their grandmother had a big surprise for them. Her dog Tiffany had just given birth to four adorable puppies! The girls named the puppies Honey, Rookie, DJ, and Taffy.

After unpacking their suitcases, the girls explored their grandmother's attic.

"What's this?" Skipper asked as she picked up a dusty scroll.

"It's my old treasure map!" Barbie exclaimed. "Every summer, Grandpa and I used to look for clues together. But after a while, we gave up." Legend told that the town's founding fathers had hidden a treasure for Willows to use, if it was ever needed.

Barbie headed out to visit her friend Christie. Skipper took a picture of the map with her tablet. Then she and her sisters decided to search for the treasure.

CITY HALL

Their first stop was city hall. Near the Willows town emblem, the sisters discovered a clue: "We came from afar, to this great land, carrying the future in the palm of our hand."

Skipper quickly searched for a picture of the founding fathers on her tablet. They were holding a vase with a twig in it. The first willow tree in Willows had grown from that twig!

"That's it!" exclaimed Skipper.

Meanwhile, Barbie couldn't wait to see Christie at Willowfest, Willows' big annual festival. But Barbie was sad to discover that the festival—along with the town—was looking a little run-down. And worst of all, Christie and her family were moving away!

Back at city hall, Barbie's sisters found the vase.
Stacie pressed the emblem at the base and a small
willow tree charm popped out!

"I'm going to borrow this, in case we need it for
the treasure hunt," Stacie said.

On the bottom of the vase they discovered their
next clue: "What runs for miles and never gets tired?"

After a while, Stacie cried, "Running water!"

"It must be Lake Willows!" the girls exclaimed.

Two Willowfest workers noticed the sisters looking at the map and also wanted the treasure.

"Maybe we should let the girls do all the work finding the clues," Joe told his friend Marty. "They'll lead us right to the treasure. Then we'll grab it."

The sisters searched near Lake Willows and found their next clue in a nearby fountain. Stacie threw a coin at the willow symbol, hitting it and causing the fountain to rise and reveal a secret inscription: "Slowly progressing like a midday chime, the growth of a tree is a reflection of time."

"The clock tower!" the sisters exclaimed.

Day after day, the sisters searched for clues near the clock tower. But they couldn't find any. Stacie hummed the tune from the clock chimes and realized that the lyrics probably held the clue. Skipper used an app to identify the song. It was called "Beneath the Willow Tree." The next clue must be under the town's famous first willow tree!

As they searched near the tree, Joe and Marty stole Skipper's bag with all their clues!

The next morning, Skipper and Chelsea were upset because their clues were missing. But Stacie exclaimed, "I'm not giving up!"

"Grandpa always said the best part of an adventure was sharing it with the people you love," Barbie told her sisters. "Let's go save Willows!"

Using the old treasure map, the girls and the pups dug near the willow tree. They found a Willows town emblem with a puzzle on it! Chelsea quickly solved it. Suddenly, the ground shook and opened to reveal . . . a tunnel!

The girls didn't get far before Joe and Marty caught up with them. "That's far enough, girls. That treasure is ours."

"Not if I can help it!" said Barbie. She made sure her sisters were clamped in. Then they swiftly rappelled to the bottom of the tunnel.

The sisters followed the tunnel to a vault. Stacie used the willow charm to open it. Diamonds, gold, and jewels sparkled before them! The puppies dove into piles of gold while Barbie and her sisters tried on tiaras and necklaces.

Suddenly, Joe and Marty appeared. The two greedy men grabbed jewels, gold, and diamonds, then tried to escape. Luckily, the pups raced after them and tied them up.

"Puppies one. Bad guys zero," said Skipper.

The next day, Barbie, her sisters, and the puppies were honored at city hall. They had donated the treasure to save the town of Willows. Part of the treasure was given to them as a reward.

Grandma Roberts had another surprise. "You know, the puppies are getting bigger. I couldn't possibly keep all of them."

"Can *we* keep them?" Chelsea asked.

"Of course," said Barbie. "They're part of the family now!"

That afternoon, the girls rode all the restored rides at Willowfest. Barbie was happy to hear that Christie's family was going to stay.

But before she and her sisters left, Barbie had had one last thing to do.

"Taffy and I planted new clues around town, and I made this new treasure map," Barbie said with a smile. "It's for the next adventurous spirit who comes to Willows!"